# BEGINNER'S
# Sewing
# & Knitting

## Helen Allen

## Illustrated by Diana McLean

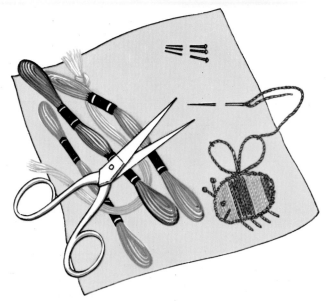

Designed by Graham Round,
Kim Blundell and Pica Design

Edited by Lisa Watts

# Contents

Diana McLean is with Linden Artists

Handlettering by J. G. McPherson

Paste-up by Terry Shannon

First published in 1979 by Usborne Publishing Ltd, 20 Garrick Street, London WC2E 9BJ, England.

Copyright © 1979 Usborne Publishing Ltd
Published in Canada by Hayes Publishing Ltd, Burlington, Ontario.

Printed in England by Hazell Watson & Viney Ltd, Aylesbury, Bucks.

# How to use this book

This book is a basic guide to the skills of needlework for absolute beginners. Simple, step-by-step instructions show you how to sew and do patchwork, appliqué and embroidery and you can teach yourself to knit too.

Once you have learned how to do basic stitches, there are lots of ideas for things you can make. Detailed picture-by-picture explanations show you exactly what to do. There are also several pages explaining how to use a dressmaking pattern.

If you want to find out how to do a particular stitch, look it up in the index. Then turn to the page and follow the pictures and instructions as you try it out. At first you may find it difficult to keep your stitches neat and even, but this gets easier with practice.

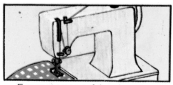

Four pages of basic guidelines explain how to use a sewing machine. There is also a special section at the back of the book which shows you what to do if the machine is not sewing properly, or the needle or thread keeps breaking.

To learn how to knit, turn to the pages near the end of the book. Clear and simple pictures show you how to do knit and purl stitches, stocking stitch and ribbing and there are instructions for things you can knit for yourself.

When you start making things on your own, or from other books and patterns, you can use this book to check how to do a special stitch or technique. At the back of the book there is a list of sewing terms with explanations you can refer to.

# Starting off

You need only a few things to begin sewing — needles and thread, fabric and scissors and some pins are useful, too. It is a good idea, though, to start collecting sewing things for when you need them. You can cut the buttons off old clothes, keep bits of tape and elastic and save scraps of fabric.

A pair of scissors with long blades are best for cutting fabric and small scissors are handy for snipping threads.

Never cut paper with sewing scissors — it blunts them.

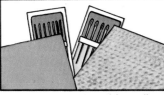

Pins are for holding fabric in position while you sew. Throw away blunt or rusty pins as they mark the fabric.

You can buy packets of needles of assorted sizes. Thin needles are for fine fabrics and thicker ones for heavier cloths.

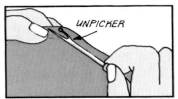

PULL THREAD THROUGH EYE

UNPICKER

A needle threader makes threading needles easier, especially if you are sewing with thick thread or knitting yarn.

An unpicker is useful for undoing mistakes. Cut through some of the stitches, then pull out the threads.

## Threading a needle

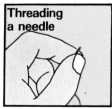

Cut or smooth the thread to make a clean, unfrayed end.

Hold the end steady and thread the eye of the needle onto it.

For thick threads, fold the end and force it through.

## Fastening on and off

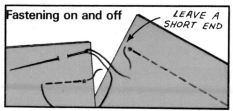

LEAVE A SHORT END

The neatest way to start or finish off a piece of thread is with tiny stitches on top of each other. You can use a knot if you like.

Make the stitches very small so the thread does not slip.

## Starting knot

Hold the end of the thread and wind it round your finger.

Slide your finger back so the thread rolls off.

Hold the loose knot between your fingers and pull it tight.

## Finishing knot

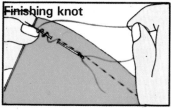
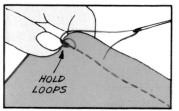

HOLD LOOPS

With the needle in the fabric, wind the thread round it three times.

Pull the needle through and hold the loops of thread against the fabric to make a knot.

# First stitches

Even if you have a sewing machine there will still be times when you have to do some handsewing. Try to keep all your stitches about the same size and with even spaces between them. Start off with a piece of thread about 60cm long. If it is longer than this it may become tangled.

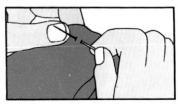

Find a comfortable position for handsewing. Support the fabric with one hand and keep the other free to make the stitches.

## Running stitch

This is for joining fabric, but it is not a very strong stitch.

Fasten the thread at the right-hand side of your work.

A little way along pick a bit of fabric up on the needle.

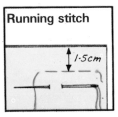

Pull the needle and thread through.

Make another stitch the same size and pull needle through.

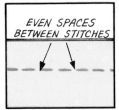

*EVEN SPACES BETWEEN STITCHES*

Stitch along like this, not pulling the thread too tight.

## Tacking

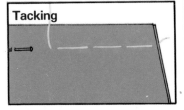

These are large running stitches for holding fabric together before you sew it properly.

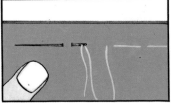

For tacking, make long stitches with small spaces between them, like this.

6

## Backstitch

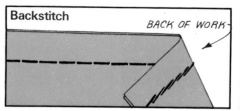

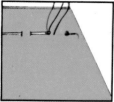

This is a strong, firm stitch for joining pieces of fabric. You start at the right-hand side of the fabric and work along.

Fasten on the thread and make a small running stitch.

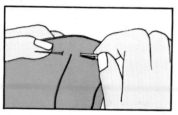

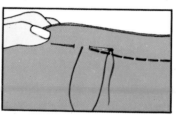

Put the needle back in the fabric at the end of the first stitch. Bring it through a little further on.

Continue making stitches like this, trying to keep them the same size.

## Hem-stitch

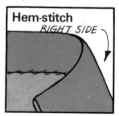

Hems are sewn so the stitches hardly show.

Start off with a knot or tiny stitches inside the hem.

Pick up a few threads just below the hem.

Then put the needle through the edge of the hem.

A little way along take another small stitch from below the hem, then put the needle through the fold and continue like this.

# More stitches

## Overstitch

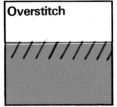  

Use this to neaten a raw edge or to join two edges.

Fasten on and work in the direction most comfortable for you.

Take the thread over the edge and put the needle in at the back.

 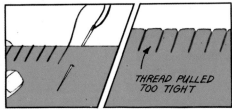

Pull the needle through, then put it in at the back again.

Continue along the edge, making stitches like this. Try not to pull the thread too tight or it will pucker the edge.

THREAD PULLED TOO TIGHT

## Blanket and . . . buttonhole* stitch

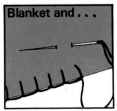  

SMALL CLOSELY SPACED STITCHES

These two are the same stitch, but different sizes. They are for neatening raw edges and can be used for decoration too.

Hold the fabric like this and fasten the thread on the left.

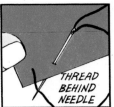  

THREAD BEHIND NEEDLE

Bring the thread forwards and put the needle in the fabric.

Pull the needle through fabric and the loop of thread.

Work other stitches like this, keeping them evenly spaced.

*For how to make buttonholes, see page 21.*

# Fabrics

Fabrics may be made of natural fibres such as cotton and wool, or from man-made fibres such as nylon. They can also be a mixture of both. Cotton is one of the easier fabrics to sew with.

Fabrics are made in several different widths: 90cm, 115cm and 160cm are the most common. You buy a piece the length you need.

When you choose a fabric, check what width it is and work out how much you will need.

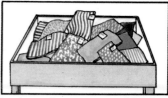

Look out for remnants of fabric which are sold at cheaper prices. These are short lengths left at the end of a roll.

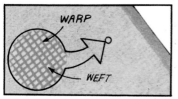

Fabric is woven from long threads called the warp and cross threads called the weft.

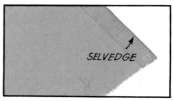

The woven, uncut edges of the fabric are called the selvedges.

If you pull fabric along the warp threads it stretches very little. This is called the straight grain of the fabric.

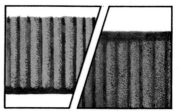

The pile of corduroy and velvet is called the nap. The nap makes the fabric look a different colour from different directions.

*More about fabrics on pages 34-35.*

# Cutting out

It is always best to use a pattern when you cut fabric, even for very simple shapes. This can either be a pattern you have made yourself*, or one you have bought*. Cut the fabric carefully — there is very little you can do if you make a mistake when you cut it.

You can make simple patterns by drawing the shapes on newspaper. Remember to allow 1.5cm all round for the seams.

Lay the fabric on a flat surface. Pin the pattern pieces so that they have a straight side along the straight grain of the fabric.

Pin all the pieces to the fabric before you start cutting. Try to position them so you do not waste much fabric.

To cut two pieces the same, fold the fabric so you cut through two thicknesses at once.

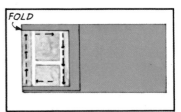

If you put one edge of a pattern on a fold you can avoid sewing that side.

On velvet or corduroy, all the pattern pieces must face the same way or they will look different colours.

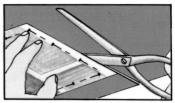

Cut round the pattern with long-bladed scissors. Hold the fabric flat with one hand and move round it. Do not move the fabric.

10  *For cutting out a dressmaking pattern see page 28.

# A bag to make

To make this small bag you need about 30cm of 90cm wide fabric and about 2m of thick cord. You could probably find a remnant big enough or a piece of fabric left over from something else.

For the pattern, cut a square 25cm × 25cm from newspaper.

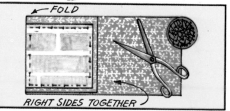

Fold fabric with right sides together and raw edges even. Pin pattern with one edge on the fold and cut round other three sides.

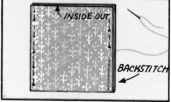

Take off the paper pattern and pin, then backstitch the side and bottom of the bag 1.5cm in from the edges.

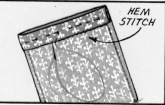

Turn the top edge over twice, keeping it even all round. Pin it and hem-stitch the edge.

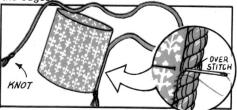

Turn bag the right way and poke out the corners. Cut cord the right length, tie knots 5cm from the ends. Stitch to bag.

Fray the ends of the cord with a pin to make tassels.

11

# Setting up a sewing machine

A sewing machine works with two threads, one from the reel on top of the machine and the other from the bobbin inside the machine. The two threads loop together to make the stitches.

You need a firm, flat surface to put your machine on, large enough for the machine and all your sewing things. If you have an electric machine, do not plug it in until you need to use it. Always put the plug into the machine before you plug it into the wall socket and when you have finished, take the plug from the wall socket before pulling the other plug out of the machine. Most modern machines are electric, but if you have a hand operated machine it is still useful.

**An electric sewing machine**

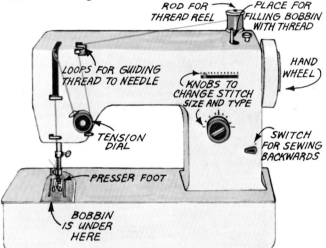

The presser foot holds the fabric in place while you sew.

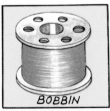

The bobbin contains thread and fits inside the machine.

This dial controls the tightness of the top thread.

## Filling the bobbin

You fill the bobbin with thread from the reel on top of the machine. Find out how to do this in your instruction manual.

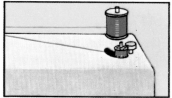

Fill the bobbin to just below the rim. If you overfill it the thread may get tangled inside the machine.

## Putting the bobbin in

The bobbin either goes into a shuttle, or straight into the machine. Find out how to fit the bobbin for your machine.

Before you put the bobbin in, make sure the needle is up. If necessary turn the hand wheel towards you to raise it.

## Threading the needle

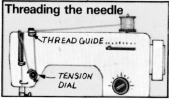

THREAD GUIDE ........

TENSION DIAL

Follow your machine instructions carefully for putting the top thread through the thread guides and round the tension dial.

Find out which way you should thread the needle for your machine, if you do it the wrong way the thread breaks.

## Raising the bobbin thread

To bring the bobbin thread out of the machine, turn the hand wheel towards you to lower the needle and raise it again.

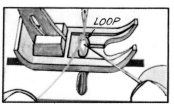

LOOP

As the needle comes up it brings a loop of bobbin thread with it. Pull the loop out with a pin so the thread runs freely.

# Sewing by machine

For most sewing jobs you need only straight stitching, but zig-zag stitches are useful for stretch fabrics, finishing off raw edges, or decoration. Most electric machines do zig-zag stitches and some embroidery as well. The stitch control knobs vary on different machines, so check how yours works.

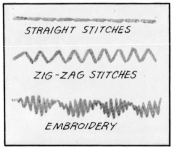

STRAIGHT STITCHES

ZIG-ZAG STITCHES

EMBROIDERY

Your machine will have a lever or dial to change the length of the stitches. Most also have a control to make it sew backwards.

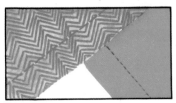

Use large stitches for thick fabrics such as wool and canvas and shorter stitches for finer fabrics.

## Zig-zag stitching

You may have to change the foot on your machine to do zig-zag stitching. Before you switch to zig-zag, make sure the needle is raised and you are using the correct presser foot.

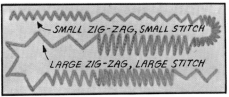

SMALL ZIG-ZAG, SMALL STITCH

LARGE ZIG-ZAG, LARGE STITCH

By adjusting the zig-zag control and the stitch length you can vary the shape of the zig-zags. Try some out on a piece of scrap fabric.

For sewing raw edges use a medium sized zig-zag stitch.

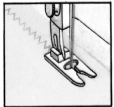

Use small-to-medium sized zig-zags for stretch fabrics.

For buttonholes use medium zig-zags and a short stitch length.

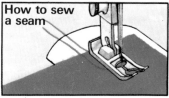

## How to sew a seam

Raise the presser foot and put the fabric so the needle is about 1cm from the end of the stitching line.

Lower the presser foot, switch the machine to reverse. Stitch back to the edge of the fabric. Switch to forward stitching.

Sew along the seam, using the edge of the presser foot as a guide to keep you straight. Hold your hands on either side of your work and do not push or pull the fabric.

At the end, sew several stitches in reverse to finish off.

To take the fabric from the machine, turn the hand wheel towards you to raise the needle, then lift the presser foot.

Pull the fabric towards the back of the machine and cut the threads close to the fabric.

## Sewing ideas

You could make a pattern with straight and zig-zag stitches on a piece of fabric and sew it to a pair of jeans.

# Seams and turnings

A seam is the place where two pieces of fabric are sewn together and a turning or hem is where the fabric is folded and stitched down to finish off a raw edge.

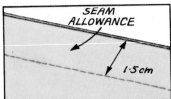

You can sew seams by machine, or by hand with a small backstitch. Hems can be sewn by machine, or by hand with hem-stitch.

When you sew a seam, your stitches should be 1.5cm from the edge of the fabric. This is called the seam allowance.

## Straight seams

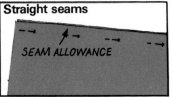

Put the two pieces of fabric together with the right sides facing each other. Pin along the side 1.5cm from the edge.

If you are going to sew the seam by machine, it is easier to tack it first (see page 6) and take out the pins before machining.

Sew along the line of tacking stitches, then pull out tacking.

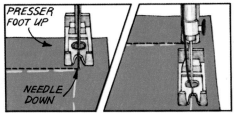

To turn a corner, leave the needle in the fabric and lift the presser foot. Turn the fabric, lower the foot and continue sewing.

## Curved seams

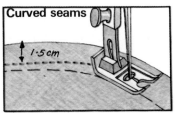

Prepare and sew in the same way as straight seams, leaving 1.5cm seam allowance.

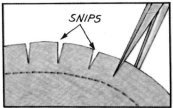

Then make snips in the seam allowance so the seam lies flat when you turn it the right way.

## Ironing

You should iron each seam after sewing it, or at least before any more stitching makes the seam difficult to reach. Frequent pressing gives sewing a much better finish.

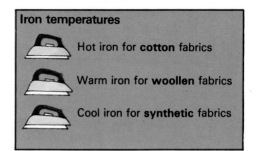

**Iron temperatures**

Hot iron for **cotton** fabrics

Warm iron for **woollen** fabrics

Cool iron for **synthetic** fabrics

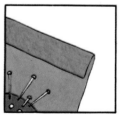

*PRESSED OPEN*

*PRESSED TO ONE SIDE*

Seams can be pressed open on both sides of the stitching, or flat to one side.

### Be careful

If you are not sure how hot an iron to use, test it on a piece of scrap fabric first.

Always unplug the iron when you are not using it.

## Hems

A hem can be a narrow turning about the width of a seam, or deeper turning for skirts and trousers. For sewing the hems of garments, see pages 32-33.

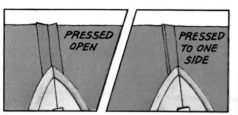

*RAW EDGE*

A hem is folded twice so the raw edge is inside.

Turn the raw edge to the wrong side of the fabric.

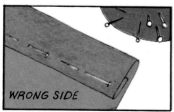

*WRONG SIDE*

Fold over again and pin, making sure the hem is the same width all the way along.

*HEM STITCH*

Then sew the hem by hand with hem-stitch, or by machine close to the inside fold.

17

# How to make a wall bag

To make this bag you need 60cm of 90cm wide fabric for the background and 40cm of 90cm wide fabric for the loops and pockets. You could choose a different coloured fabric for the loops and pockets, as in the picture.

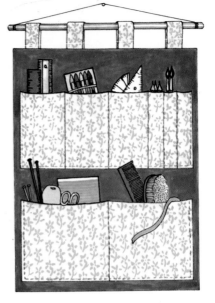

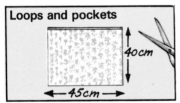

**Loops and pockets**

40cm

←45cm→

Fold the 40cm length of fabric in half widthways and cut along the fold to make two pieces.

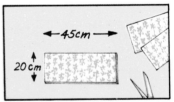

←45cm→

20cm

Fold both pieces in half again and cut along the folds. This makes two pieces for pockets, one for loops and a spare piece.

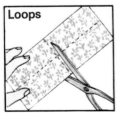

**Loops**

Cut one piece in half lengthways and crossways.

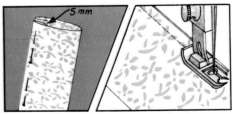

5mm

Fold the loops lengthways, tuck in about 5mm and pin the sides together. Sew down the side of each loop, keeping near the edge.

## Background

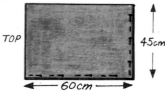

TOP

60cm

45cm

POKE GENTLY

Fold the 60cm length of fabric in half with the right sides together. Pin along the bottom and side, then machine or backstitch.

Turn the bag the right way, poke out the corners and iron.

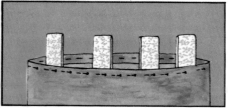

Turn the top edge in 1.5cm and pin it. Then fold the loops in half and pin them spaced evenly along the top with their ends inside.

Tack along the top of the bag through all the thicknesses.

### Pockets

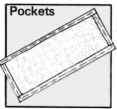

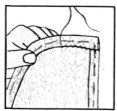

Sew across the top of the bag keeping close to the edge.

Turn the edges under 1.5cm and tack them down.

Turn the top edges down another 1.5cm and hem-stitch them.

Pin the pockets in position on the background, tack, then sew round leaving them open at the top.

Pin down the pockets where you want them divided, then stitch along the lines of pins.

# Buttons, hooks and press studs

When you sew on buttons, hooks or press studs it is quicker to use a double piece of thread. To do this, thread the needle and pull the ends to the same length. Fasten on with a knot or stitches.

**Buttons**

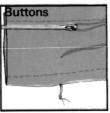

Fasten on at the back and bring the needle to the front.

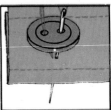

Put needle in one hole and back through another.

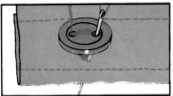

Sew through the button about six times, leaving the thread quite loose so the button is not tight on the fabric.

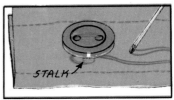

STALK

Bring needle through to front of fabric. Wind the thread several times behind the button to make a short stalk. Fasten off.

**Thick fabrics**

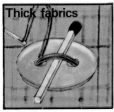

Sew like this so the button is not sewn on too tightly.

**Four holes**

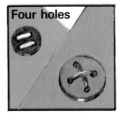

You can sew these on in either of these two ways.

**Buttons with shanks**

SHANK
STALK

These have a loop on the back and need only a short stalk.

**Hooks and eyes**

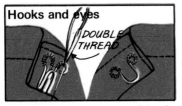

DOUBLE THREAD

Sew these on the wrong side of the fabric with overstitches. The hook and loop go on the edge of the fabric.

**Press studs**

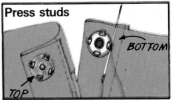

BOTTOM
TOP

With small overstitches sew the bottom stud to the right side of the fabric and the top stud to the wrong side.

20

# How to make buttonholes

Strong buttonholes on thick fabrics go at right angles to the edge. On thinner fabrics, put them parallel to the edge.

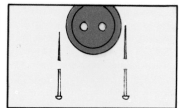

Mark the size for the buttonhole with pins. It should be a bit wider than the button.

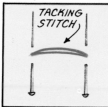

Do a large tacking stitch to mark the place for the hole.

Mark the shape for the buttonhole with running stitches.

Carefully cut the fabric along the large tacking stitch.

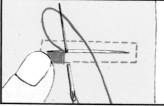

Do buttonhole stitch* round the hole. Start on the inner edge for horizontal holes and at the bottom for vertical holes.

When you reach the end of the first side, work the stitches round in the shape of a fan.

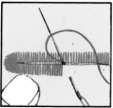

Work back down the other side of the hole.

At the other end do several long stitches across the hole.

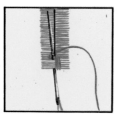

Do buttonhole stitch over the long stitches. Fasten off.

*See page 8 for how to do buttonhole stitch.

21

# How to put in a zip

You should always pin and tack a zip in place before sewing it, to make sure it is straight and lying flat. If you are dressmaking, it is best to sew the zip at the same time as the seam. To replace a broken zip, sew up the opening with tacking stitches before laying the zip in position.

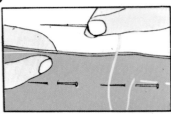

If you are dressmaking, pin then tack along the seam in which the zip goes.

Mark the length of the zip on the seam with a pin.

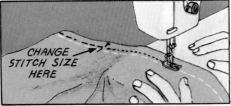

Starting at the top, sew the seam as far as the pin with the largest machine stitch. Then continue with a normal stitch size.

Press the seam open and remove tacking if you are dressmaking.

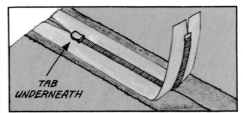

Lay the zip on the seam with the tab facing the fabric and the teeth along the join of the seam.

Pin the zip carefully at the bottom.

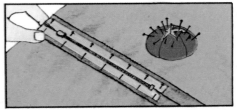

Put pins all along the zip, as shown in the picture. Make sure the fabric lies flat and the zip is straight along the seam line.

Tack down both sides of the zip and across the bottom.

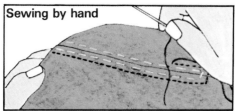

### Sewing by hand

Sew the zip on the right side of the fabric, using small backstitches and keeping about 7mm from the line of the seam.

ZIP FOOT

Put the zip foot on the machine and slide it to the left.

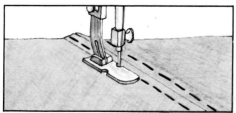

Position the fabric with the right side up and the needle about 7mm to the left of the seam. Sew all round the zip.

Press the zip on the wrong side. Do not iron nylon teeth.

Pull out all the tacking stitches.

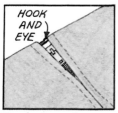

HOOK AND EYE

You may need a hook and eye (see p.20) at the top.

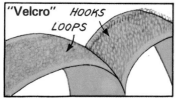

"Velcro" HOOKS LOOPS

This is another way to fasten openings. It is two strips of nylon, one with little hooks and the other with tiny loops.

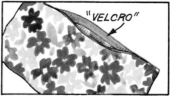

"VELCRO"

Pin one strip of "Velcro" along each side of the opening and sew by hand or machine down both sides of the strips.

# Binding edges

Instead of a hem you can sew special tape to a raw edge to finish it off. This tape is called bias binding and you can buy it in sewing shops. Bias means cut at an angle to the straight grain. Fabric cut on the bias stretches a little, so you can ease the tape round curves and corners.

These things are lined with stiff or padded interfacing. On the opposite page you can find out how to use interfacing.

## How to use bias binding

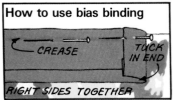

Open up one of the folds of the bias binding. Place the binding along the edge of the fabric and pin along the crease of the fold.

When you reach a corner, make a triangular-shaped fold to take the binding neatly round the corner.

Machine or backstitch binding to fabric along the crease.

Iron the binding up towards the edge of the fabric.

Fold binding over edge of fabric. Pin and hem-stitch.

## Interfacing

This is a material which you put between two layers of fabric to give it more body. You can buy plain or padded interfacing. Plain interfacing such as "Vilene" comes in several degrees of stiffness. You can also get iron-on "Vilene" which sticks to the fabric when you press it with a warm iron.

Cut stiff or padded interfacing the same size as your pattern pieces.

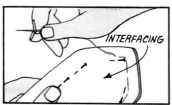

Tack the interfacing to the wrong side of one of the pieces of fabric to be lined. Pull the tacking out later.

For the iron-on interfacing, put the shiny side against the wrong side of the fabric and press with a warm iron.

### Small purse

Draw this shape on a folded piece of paper and cut it out.

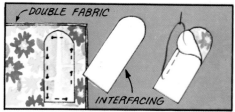

Unfold the pattern and cut it once from stiff interfacing and twice from fabric. Attach interfacing to wrong side of one fabric piece.

Tack the two pieces of fabric together, right sides out.

Bind the edges with bias binding, as described on page 24.

Fold the purse like this and stitch close to the binding.

## Padded glasses case

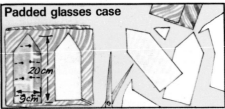

Draw and cut a paper pattern for the case. Cut the pattern four times from fabric and twice from padded interfacing.

Tack padding to the wrong side of each of two fabric pieces.

Tack each padded piece of fabric to an unpadded piece.

Now sew binding round the edges of each piece.

Pin the two sides of the case together and sew up the sides.

## Wallet

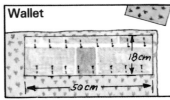

Make a paper pattern the sizes shown above and cut the pattern twice from fabric and once from stiff interfacing.

Attach interfacing to the wrong side of one piece of fabric. Put the two pieces of fabric together and pin the ends.

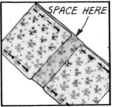

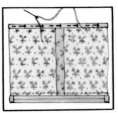

Sew the ends only. Turn the fabric the right way and press.

Fold the ends over like this and pin along the sides.

Sew the binding to the top and bottom of the wallet.

# Gathering and elastic

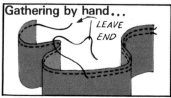
**Gathering by hand...** *LEAVE END*

To gather fabric to make a frill do two lines of running stitches with pieces of thread long enough to reach the end.

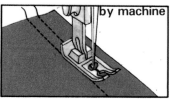
**by machine**

With the longest straight stitch, sew along 1.5cm from the edge of the fabric. Do a second row a little bit nearer the edge.

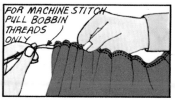
*FOR MACHINE STITCH PULL BOBBIN THREADS ONLY*

Pull the fabric along the threads to gather it up. When it is the right length, tie the threads securely together.

*RIGHT SIDES TOGETHER*

Spread the gathers evenly along the threads, then pin to the main fabric and sew together below the lower gathering line.

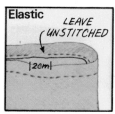
**Elastic** *LEAVE UNSTITCHED* |2cm|

Sew a hem wide enough to thread the elastic through.

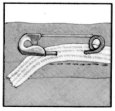

Safety pin one end of the elastic to the hem.

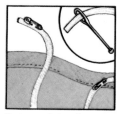

Put a safety pin or a needle called a bodkin on other end.

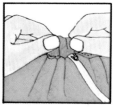

Push the pin or bodkin through hem to thread elastic.

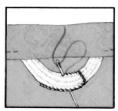

Pull the elastic to the right size, cut the end and sew.

Sew up the opening in the hem.

# Dressmaking 1

When you first start dressmaking choose a pattern for a simple style. Check that the fabric you want is suitable for the pattern. If you want velvet, corduroy, a fabric with a one-way design, or wish to match the design at the seams, ask the shop assistant how much extra fabric you should buy.

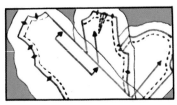

Each pattern usually has several styles, so sort out the pieces you need and press them with a cool iron.

Check your measurements to see if you need to alter the pattern. To shorten it, fold along the lines marked on the pieces.

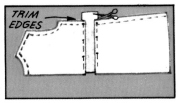

To lengthen a pattern piece, cut it along the lines and pin a piece of paper in the gap to make it the right length.

## Cutting out

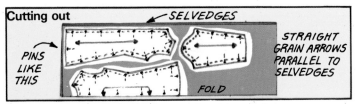

To pin the pattern to the fabric, carefully follow the instructions for your size and style. Lay the fabric on a large, flat surface and make sure there are no creases or wrinkles. If it is supposed to be folded, the right sides should be together.

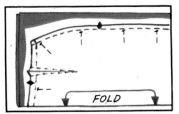

Pieces marked with an arrow like this should be placed on the fold of the fabric. Do not cut the fold.

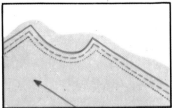

If there is only one pattern for several sizes, be careful to cut round the line for your size.

## Velvet and corduroy

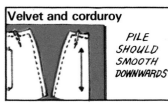

*PILE SHOULD SMOOTH DOWNWARDS*

The pile, or nap, of the fabric must face the same way in every pattern piece or they will look different colours.

## Patterned fabric

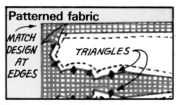

*MATCH DESIGN AT EDGES*

*TRIANGLES*

To match a design at the seams, make sure the little triangles on the pattern pieces are on the same part of the design.

*CUT THROUGH PAPER*

Check that all the pattern pieces are pinned correctly to the fabric. Then cut round them with long-bladed scissors.

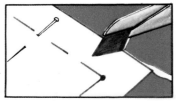

Cut carefully round the outside of the little triangles. These help you pin the fabric together correctly.

## Tailor's tacks

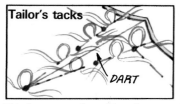

*DART*

This is a way of marking the fabric with information from the pattern, such as the position of darts, buttonholes and buttons.

*LONG ENDS*

To make tailor's tacks, thread the needle with a long thread and pull the ends the same length. Make a small stitch.

*LEAVE LONG ENDS*

Make another stitch and leave a loop. Cut the thread.

Mark everything you need then carefully pull off the pattern. Gently pull the two layers of fabric apart and cut threads between them.

# Dressmaking 2

The explanations given on these two pages should make the instructions in your pattern easy to follow.

For best results tack all the seams before sewing them and keep trying on the garment to see if you need to alter it. Remember to iron all seams before more stitching makes them hard to reach.

**Stay-stitching**

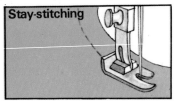

This is a line of machine stitches round curved edges to stop them stretching before the pieces are sewn together.

**Darts**

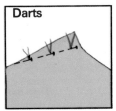

Match tailor's tacks and pin darts on the wrong side.

Tack along the dart, tapering it to a fine point.

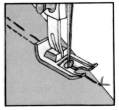

Machine down beside the line of tacking.

**Sewing pieces together**

TRIANGLES

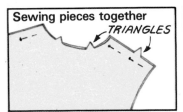

Pin the pieces right sides together and make sure the triangles on both pieces line up.

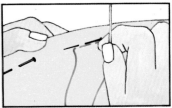

Tack along the seams, then try the garment on to make sure it fits and alter if necessary.

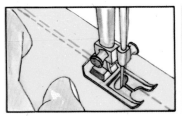

Then sew the seams by machine, keeping as straight as possible.

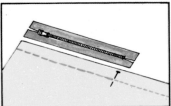

To find out how to fit a zip, see page 22.

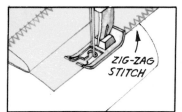

If you are sewing a fabric that frays a lot you could overstitch or zig-zag the raw edges.

Press all the seams flat, either open or to one side according to the instructions in the pattern.

## Interfacing

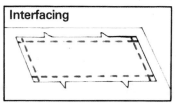

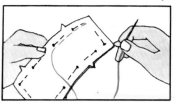

For pieces that need stiffening with interfacing*, use the pattern piece to cut the shape from the interfacing.

Attach the interfacing to the wrong side of the fabric.

## Facings

These are pieces of fabric sewn to raw edges to finish them.

Pin the facing to the raw edge, right sides of fabric together.

Tack, then sew, the facing to the garment.

If it is a curved seam, make snips in the seam allowance.

Press the facing to the wrong side of the garment.

Turn under the edge of the facing and stitch to garment.

*More about interfacing on page 25.

31

# How to turn up hems

Turning up or letting down a hem is easy if the hem is already straight, but if it is not you will have to measure round it to get a straight line. Even on shop-bought clothes, hems are often not straight. Try on the garment lots of times before cutting away any fabric.

First decide how long you want the garment and pin it up roughly to that length.

Mark the length with a pin and let down the hem. Ask someone to mark the length all round by measuring it from the floor.

Fold up the hem, pin it, then tack round the fold. The easiest place to work is at an ironing board.

Put a line of pins 7cm from the fold all round the hem.

Cut along the line of pins to make a 7cm deep hem.

Turn under the top of the hem and tack it to the skirt.

Sew round the hem with hem-stitch using thread which matches the colour of the fabric.

Pull out the tacking, then press the lower edge of the hem only.

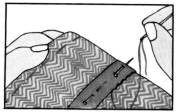

Sew bias binding* to the raw edge of the hem as the fabric is too bulky to turn over twice.

Fold the binding up and hem-stitch it to the skirt.

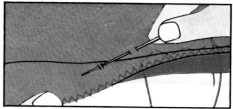

Instead of binding, you could zig-zag round the raw edge.

Then turn up the hem and sew it by folding back the edge and taking small stitches from inside the hem and the skirt.

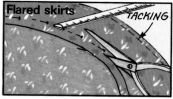

Prepare the hem of a flared skirt in the normal way, cutting the fabric to leave a hem 7cm deep.

Do a line of running stitches round the top of the hem. Pull the thread to gather the hem so it fits the skirt.

Sew bias binding on to the gathered edge of the hem.

Fold over the binding and hem-stitch it to the skirt.

Press the lower edge of the hem only.

*For how to use bias binding see page 24.

# Different kinds of fabrics

When you choose a fabric to buy, check what it is made of and how you should wash and iron it. It may say on the label, or you can ask the shop assistant.

Some fabrics are much easier to work with than others. Very thick or very thin fabrics, shiny fabrics and those with a nap need special care.

## Thick and thin fabrics

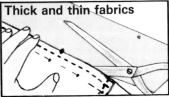

Be careful that thin fabrics such as voile and organdie do not slip when you are cutting them. Sew with a fine needle and thread.

Sew thick fabrics such as tweed with a large needle and long stitches. Be careful of loosely woven fabrics which fray.

## Stretchy fabrics

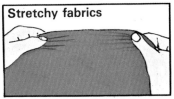

Take care not to stretch jersey, velour or stretch towelling when you cut it out. If you do the pieces will be cut wrongly.

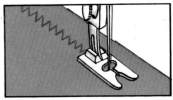

Sew with "stretch stitch" if your machine does it. If not, use a zig-zag stitch, or a medium sized straight stitch.

## Fabrics that fray

After sewing the seams you can trim them with special scissors called pinking shears.

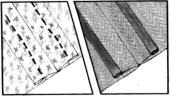

Instead of trimming the seams you could turn over the raw edges of thin fabrics, or bind thick fabrics with bias binding.

## Fabrics with nap or pile

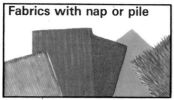

These include velvet, corduroy, needlecord, velour and fake-fur fabrics.

If you use a pile fabric for dressmaking, the pile should always smooth downwards.

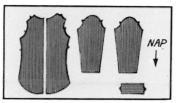

Remember to cut all the pattern pieces with the nap going in the same direction.

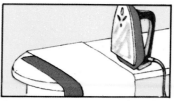

Press corduroy, needlecord and velour on the wrong side with a damp cloth, but do not iron velvet.

## Stripes and one-way designs

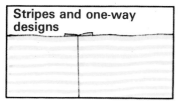

If you are using fabric which has stripes or checks you need extra fabric so you can match the design at the seams.

You will also need extra fabric to keep a one-way design the right way up in all the pattern pieces.

## Thread

This can be made of cotton or synthetic fibres. Use cotton for natural fabrics such as wool and cotton and synthetic thread for man-made fabrics.

For most sewing, thread No. 40 is the right thickness. You can also buy thick thread for sewing buttonholes and nylon thread for sewing hems invisibly.

# How to do appliqué

This is a way of decorating fabric by sewing shaped patches onto it. The patches can be made of any fabric but felt is the easiest as it does not fray so you do not have to hem the edges. Choose a firm fabric, such as thick cotton, for the background.

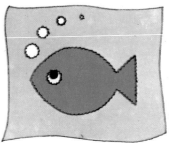

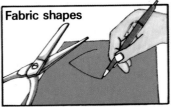

**Fabric shapes**

Draw a simple shape on the fabric and cut it out, allowing about 5mm for turning under the edges.

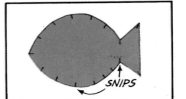

SNIPS

Make snips 3mm deep along the curves and in the corners of the shape.

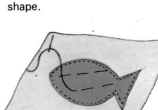

5mm TURNING

Turn the edges over about 5mm and tack all the way round.

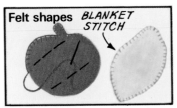

Tack the shape on the background fabric with a few large stitches.

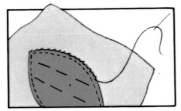

Then hem-stitch the shape securely to the background fabric and pull out the tacking.

**Felt shapes** BLANKET STITCH

You can sew these straight on the background fabric with blanket stitch.

# Appliqué ideas

If you appliqué shapes on clothes or houshold things, make sure the colours in the fabrics are fast and will not run when you wash them.

## How to hang an appliqué picture

Hem round the edges of the background fabric. Turn the top over another 5cm and hem it.

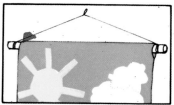

Put a stick through the top hem and tie a piece of string to both ends.

# Patchwork

By sewing small pieces of fabric together you can make a larger piece of cloth with a striking pattern. You can make patchwork from square patches, or from hexagons, triangles or other geometric shapes. It is better to use patches of one kind of fabric, cotton is the easiest, in one patchwork.

## Square patches

You need a square of card, about 8cm × 8cm to use as a pattern for the patches.

Draw carefully round the card on scraps of fabric and cut out lots of squares. Put one side of the square on the straight grain.

### Making a pattern

Next arrange the patches together so that the different fabrics make a pattern in the finished patchwork. You could put dark coloured patches next to light coloured ones, or patterned fabrics next to plain colours.

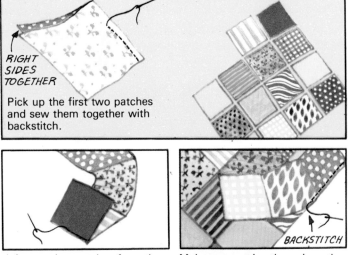

RIGHT SIDES TOGETHER

Pick up the first two patches and sew them together with backstitch.

Join on other patches from the first row of your pattern to make a strip of patchwork.

BACKSTITCH

Make more strips then pin and sew them together, carefully matching the seam lines.

## Hexagons and triangles

To cut triangular or hexagonal patches it is best to buy a plastic or metal pattern, called a template, from a sewing shop or department store. You also need some thick paper.

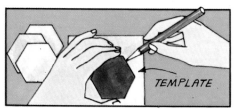

Carefully draw round the template on thick paper and cut out lots of paper shapes.

Pin the paper shapes to scraps of fabric. Lay one side of the shape along the straight grain.

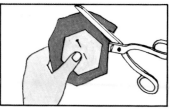

Trim the fabric about 10mm outside the paper shape.

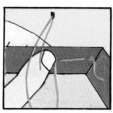

Turn over the edges of the fabric and tack to the paper.

Fold the corners over neatly so they do not bulge.

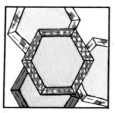

Tack round all the shapes, keeping the outline accurate.

### How to fold corners of triangles

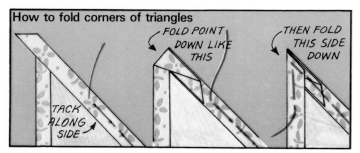

TACK ALONG SIDE

FOLD POINT DOWN LIKE THIS

THEN FOLD THIS SIDE DOWN

## Making a pattern

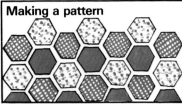
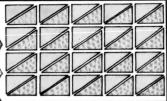

When you have made lots of patches, arrange them together to make a pattern.

You could do this on a tray so you need not disturb them if you do not finish them at one time.

## Sewing hexagons together

Pick up two patches and hold them right sides together.

Stitch along one side with tiny overstitches. Be careful not to sew through the paper as well.

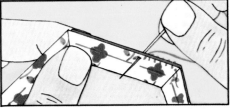

Join on other patches picking them up in order from your pattern.

### Sewing triangles

SEW LONG SIDES TOGETHER

Sew triangles together to make squares. Join the squares to make rows, then sew the rows together.

## Finishing off

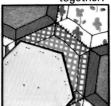

Pull out the tacking stitches holding the papers.

Lift the paper out of each patch.

Press the patchwork carefully on the wrong side.

# Things to make with patchwork

Below you can find out how to make patchwork cushions. You could also try making the bag on page 11 from a piece of patchwork, lining it with interfacing and another piece of fabric.

SQUARE PATCHES

PIN CUSHION— STUFF FIRMLY

TRIANGULAR PATCHES

HEXAGONAL PATCHES

For the back of a cushion you need a piece of fabric the same size as the patchwork.

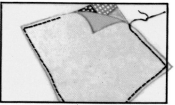

Pin the patchwork and backing fabric right sides together and machine or backstitch, leaving part of one side open.

Turn the cushion the right way round, poke out the corners and stuff with kapok bought from a shop..

OVER STITCH

Tuck in the edges of the open side and sew along it with small overstitches.

# Embroidery

You can embroider any fabric, but the best to work on is loosely woven fabric like hessian. You can also buy special embroidery fabrics such as glenshee or crash. There are lots of kinds of embroidery thread. *Coton à Broder* and pearl cotton are easiest to start with, using crewel needles size 6.

This comes in skeins. To use it, pull off the papers.

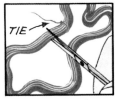

Carefully open the skein and cut it near the tie.

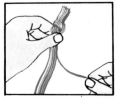

Tie a knot at one end and cut lengths as you need them.

## Embroidery stitches

There are hundreds of embroidery stitches, but many of them are variations of simple stitches. On the opposite page, all the stitches shown in one colour are based on the same simple stitch. You can find out how to do the simple stitches on this page and page 44, then you can work out the variations or make up your own.

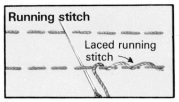

### Running stitch

This is the same as ordinary running stitch shown on page 6. For the laced stitch, thread another colour through the stitches

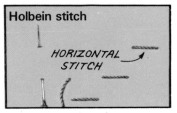

### Holbein stitch

This is a stepped pattern made with running stitches. Do the horizontal stitches first.

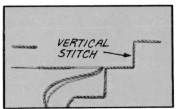

Then go back and fill in the vertical stitches.

42

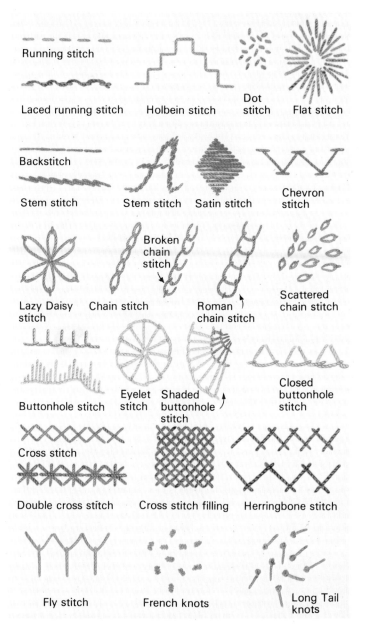

Running stitch

Laced running stitch

Holbein stitch

Dot stitch

Flat stitch

Backstitch

Stem stitch

Stem stitch

Satin stitch

Chevron stitch

Lazy Daisy stitch

Chain stitch

Broken chain stitch

Roman chain stitch

Scattered chain stitch

Buttonhole stitch

Eyelet stitch

Shaded buttonhole stitch

Closed buttonhole stitch

Cross stitch

Double cross stitch

Cross stitch filling

Herringbone stitch

Fly stitch

French knots

Long Tail knots

# Embroidery stitches

## Backstitch

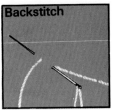

Work this in the same way as for backstitch page 7.

## Satin stitch

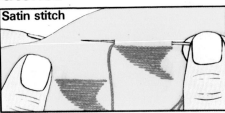

This is lots of backstitches worked close together. It is useful for making shapes or filling in areas.

## Stem stitch

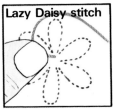

To do this make a stitch to the right. Bring the needle up again half-way back along the stitch.

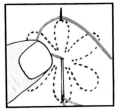

KEEP THREAD THIS SIDE OF NEEDLE

Make another stitch to the right and bring the needle up again at the end of the first stitch.

## Lazy Daisy stitch

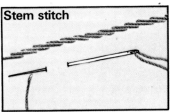

With the needle on the right side, make a loop of thread.

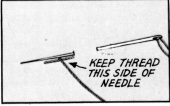

Put needle in where it came up, then out through loop.

Make a small stitch to hold the loop.

## Chain stitch

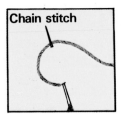

Start off in the same way as for Lazy Daisy stitch.

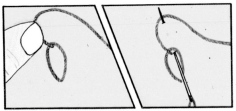

Pull the needle through and make another loop. Put the needle back inside the first loop and up again through the second loop.

## Buttonhole stitch

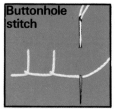

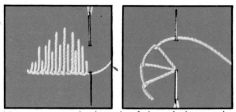

Find out how to do buttonhole stitch on page 8.

You can vary the length of the stitches and the spaces between them, or work them round in a circle to make an Eyelet stitch.

## Fly stitch

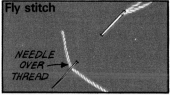

NEEDLE OVER THREAD

Make a loop of thread towards you. Put the needle in on the right and bring it through again over the loop of thread.

Do a stitch towards you and bring the needle out again at the top of the first "V" ready to start another stitch.

## Cross stitch

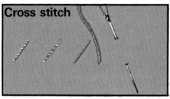

Work a line of diagonal stitches to the right. Be careful to keep them level and the same length.

Then work back making diagonal stitches in the opposite direction to finish the crosses.

## French knots

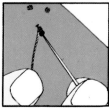

Twist the thread three times round the needle.

Put the needle back in the fabric where the thread came out.

Hold thread against the fabric and pull the needle through.

# Designs to embroider

You can make up your own embroidery designs, or buy transfers from a sewing shop. These are design outlines which you iron onto your fabric and then embroider. For your own designs you need to draw the picture on paper and work out what stitches you could use.

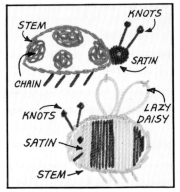

These are some designs showing which stitches you should use if you want to embroider them.

To copy the design on to fabric, trace these outlines then follow the instructions given below.

## Copying a design

Trace the outline and pin the tracing to the fabric.

Stitch through the tracing with small running stitches.

Then carefully tear off the tracing.

## Ideas for pockets

Make rows of chain stitch worked close together.

Do the outline in stem stitch and fill in with satin stitch.

Do an outline of chain stitch and fill with stem stitch.

46

# Embroidery picture

You could copy this embroidery picture, following the guide to stitches shown below, or make up your own design.

Work out the design on paper first, then draw it lightly in pencil on hessian or a special embroidery fabric.

## Stitch guide

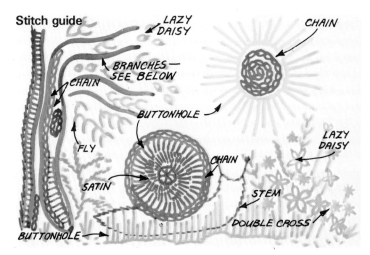

For the tree trunk you could lay pieces of knitting yarn on the fabric and stitch over them with *Coton à Broder.* This is called couching. You can use lots of different kinds of thread in one picture and sew on sequins and beads too.

# How to knit

There are two main knitting stitches — knit stitch and purl stitch. All the other stitches are variations of these two.

Making the first stitches is called casting on.

Casting on

Make a loop of yarn.

Pull the yarn through this loop to make another loop.

Put the loop on a knitting needle and pull to tighten it.

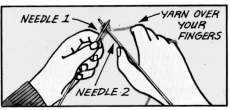

NEEDLE 1 — YARN OVER YOUR FINGERS

NEEDLE 2

Put the second needle into the back of the loop and hold the yarn and needles like this. Now you are ready to make your first stitch.

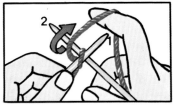

With the yarn over your finger take it under needle 2, then between the two needles.

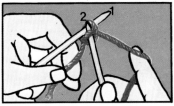

Pull needle 2 back and with the point of the needle pull the yarn through the loop on needle 1.

Put the loop which is on needle 2 onto needle 1.

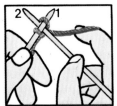

Next put needle 2 between the two loops on needle 1.

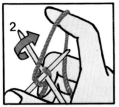

With your finger, wind the yarn round needle 2 again.

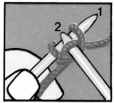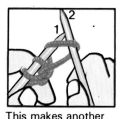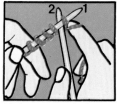

Pull it between the two stitches on needle 1.

This makes another stitch to put on needle 1.

Make more stitches like this and put them on needle 1.

## How to do knit stitch

Cast on about 20 stitches, then put needle 2 into the first stitch on needle 1.

Wind the yarn under needle 2 and out between the two needles.

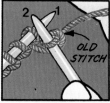

Pull the yarn through the stitch on needle 1.

Then slip the stitch off needle 1.

OLD STITCH

Put needle 2 into the next stitch and wind the yarn round.

Pull the yarn through the stitch and slip it off needle 1.

Continue along the row knitting all the stitches onto needle 2.

To start a new row move the full needle to your other hand.

## Casting off

Knit two stitches, then put needle 1 into the first stitch.

Lift the first stitch over the second one and off the needles.

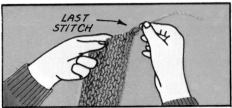

Knit another stitch.

Then lift the other stitch over it and off the needles.

Continue like this until there is only one stitch left. Cut the yarn, put the end through the stitch and pull it tight.

LAST STITCH

## Purl stitch

To do purl, cast on about 20 stitches, then hold the needles with the wool coming from the front.
Knitting that is either all knit stitches or all purl is called garter stitch.

WOOL IN FRONT

Put needle 2 into the front of the first stitch.

Wind the yarn round needle 2.

Then pull it through the stitch on needle 1.

Slip the stitch off needle 1.

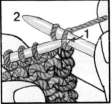

Do all the stitches on this row like this.

# Stocking stitch

This is made by knitting one row and purling the next.

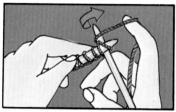

Cast on about 20 stitches, then do the first row in knit stitch.

For the next row, purl all the stitches.

When the knitting looks like this, knit the row.

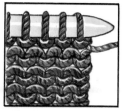

When this side is facing you, purl the row.

## Dropped stitches

It is a good idea to count your stitches from time to time. You may find you have dropped a stitch without noticing. To pick up a stitch again, work along the row until you are above the dropped stitch.

Put another needle, or a crochet hook, into the dropped stitch, from front to back for a knit stitch and from back to front for a purl.

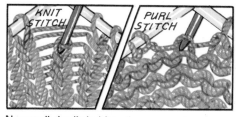

Now pull the little bits of yarn one by one through the stitch with the needle. Make sure it is the right way for knit and purl.

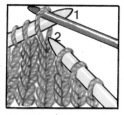

When the stitch is at the top, put it on needle 1 and knit it.

## Joining new yarn

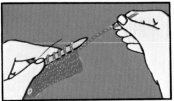

When you get near the end of a ball of yarn, do not start a new row if the yarn is not long enough to finish that row.

Start knitting the new row with the new yarn. Hold the old end and the end of the new yarn in your left hand.

Knit all along the row, then stop and tie the loose ends together. Leave the ends to sew in later.

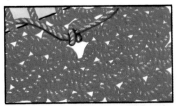

Never join yarn in the middle of a row as it makes a bump and a small hole in the knitting.

### Knitting needles

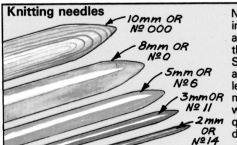

10mm OR № OOO
8mm OR № O
5mm OR № 6
3mm OR № 11
2 mm OR № 14

Needles are measured in millimetres, or by a number describing their thickness. Some of the sizes are shown on the left. Thick needles make loose knitting which grows more quickly than that done on finer needles.

### Yarn

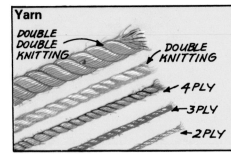

DOUBLE DOUBLE KNITTING
DOUBLE KNITTING
4 PLY
3 PLY
2 PLY

Yarn is made from several threads spun together. A yarn with three threads is called three-ply and thicker yarn is called double knitting. It can be made of wool, cotton, nylon or acrylic or a mixture of these.

# Stripy scarf to knit

This scarf is in garter stitch which means every row is done in knit stitch. You can find out how to make tassels on page 56.

## What you need

1 pair of 6½mm (No. 3) knitting needles
16 × 25gm balls of different coloured double knitting yarn

Cast on 50 stitches.

Slip the first stitch onto needle 2 without knitting it.

Then knit all along the row.

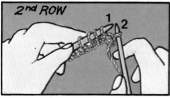

Slip the first stitch onto needle 2 then knit the row. Continue like this, slipping the first stitch of each row.

When you have knitted about 8cm join on another coloured yarn to make a stripe.

Continue knitting in the same way, changing the yarn when you want a stripe.

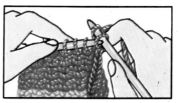

When the scarf is the length you want it, cast off. Turn to page 57 to find out how to sew in the loose ends.

## Ribbing

This is done by alternately knitting and purling the stitches along the row. It makes stretchy knitting which is good for cuffs and other edges. Cast on 20 stitches to try it out.

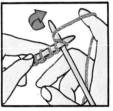

Knit the first stitch.

Then bring the yarn between the needles to the front.

Purl the next stitch.

Take the yarn back between the needles and knit the next stitch. Work along the row alternately knitting and purling the stitches.

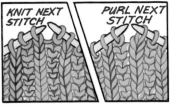

Keep count of where to knit or purl, or look at the stitches to see which you should do next.

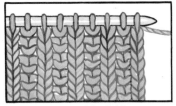

The ridges on this ribbing are one stitch wide. You can also make them two or three stitches wide.

### Tight and loose knitting

If it is difficult to put the needle in the stitch, and the stitches will not push along the needle, try not to pull the yarn so tight.

You should pull the yarn a bit tighter if the stitches are very loose and keep falling off the needles.

## Changing the shape of your knitting

To make knitting change shape you have to increase or decrease the number of stitches on the needle. Increasing makes the knitting wider and decreasing makes it narrower.

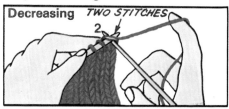

**Decreasing** *TWO STITCHES*

Put needle 2 into two stitches at the same time and knit them together.

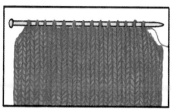

When you decrease at both ends of each row the knitting grows like this.

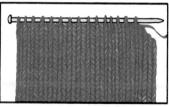

If you decrease at the beginning of every other row, the knitting slopes on one side only.

### Increasing

This is done by knitting twice into the same stitch. If you are doing stocking stitch it is easier to increase on only the knit rows.

Put the needle into the first stitch and wind the yarn round.

Pull yarn through stitch. Do not slip stitch off needle 1.

Now put needle 2 into the back of the stitch on needle 1.

Wind the yarn round needle 2 and pull it through stitch again.

Slip the stitch off needle 1 and knit along the row.

# How to make tassels

Wind some yarn lots of times round a small book.

Cut carefully along one side to make lots of lengths of yarn.

Take two lengths and fold them in half.

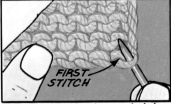

FIRST STITCH

Slip a crochet hook, or a knitting needle, through the back of the first stitch on the edge of the knitting.

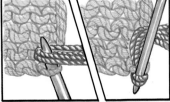

Put the yarn over the needle or hook, hold the ends firmly and pull the loop through the stitch.

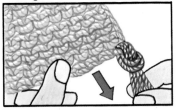

Thread the ends of the yarn through the loop and pull them to tighten it.

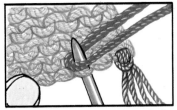

Put a tassel in every other stitch along the edge of the scarf.

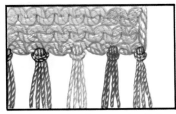

You can make the tassels all the same colour, or lots of different colours.

If the fringe is ragged at the ends, carefully trim off the long threads.

## Finishing off

When you have finished a piece of knitting you need to sew in any loose ends.

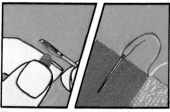

Thread one of the ends through a large-eyed needle.

Sew the end loosely in and out of the edge of the knitting. Finish off with small stitches.

Cut the yarn and sew in any other ends, being careful not to pull the yarn too tightly.

### Stitching together

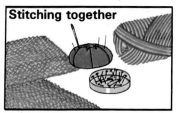

Sew pieces of knitting together with matching yarn and a large-eyed needle.

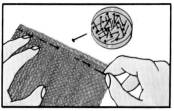

Put the pieces right sides together and pin along close to the edge.

BACKSTITCH

Thread the needle with yarn and sew along the edge with medium sized backstitches (see page 7).

DAMP COTTON CLOTH

Check whether you can use an iron on the yarn—it usually says on the wrapper.

# Leg-warmers to knit

You could knit these leg-warmers in the same yarn as the scarf on page 53 so they make a set.

### What you need

8 × 25gm balls of different coloured double knitting yarn
1 pair of 4½mm needles
1 pair of 5½mm needles
Tape-measure and row counter, or pencil and paper

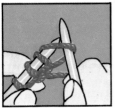

With the 4½mm needles cast on 72 stitches.

For the next row knit one stitch, purl one stitch alternately along the row. Work like this until the knitting is about 12cm long.

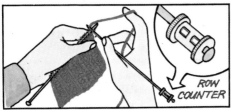

Now replace the empty needle with a 5½mm needle and rib the next row. Then with both 5½mm needles, rib seven rows.

At the end of the next row, knit two stitches together.

Carry on knitting in rib. At each end of every eighth row knit two stitches together. You can count the rows with a row counter, or mark them on a piece of paper.

Be careful to knit and purl the correct stitches.

When there are only 42 stitches left, cast off loosely.

## Finishing off

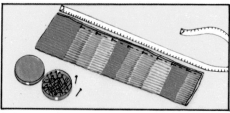

Knit the second leg-warmer, then sew in the loose ends.

Fold each piece lengthways and pin the sides together, leaving 8cm open at the wide end. Backstitch along the sides with yarn.

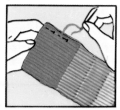

Turn the other way out and pin the last 8cm.

Sew along the line of pins to the top.

## Hints on using a knitting pattern

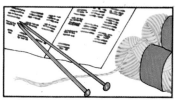

It is best to buy all the yarn you need at one time. If you buy more later it may be a slightly different colour.

Make sure you use the needles and yarn described in the pattern. Other yarn may come out a different size.

| | |
|---|---|
| k = | knit stitch |
| p = | purl stitch |
| st = | stitch |
| rep = | repeat |
| st.st. = | stocking stitch |
| g.st. = | garter stitch |

Before you start, put circles round the instructions for your size so you can spot them easily.

Read through the abbreviations, some of which are shown above, and make sure you understand them.

# Sewing machine faults

Here are some of the points you should check if your machine is not sewing properly: To test the stitches, use a scrap of fabric you are working on, folded to make a double thickness. First of all though, check that you have threaded the machine correctly.

### Needle breaks

The needle may have been blunt or bent, or too thin for the thread and fabric you were using. Check also that the tension on the top thread is not too tight. Make sure the new needle is the right size and that you put it in correctly.

### Top thread breaks

You may not have threaded the machine correctly, or the needle may be blunt, bent or too fine for the thread. If it is none of these, check that the tension on the top thread is not too tight.

### Bobbin thread breaks

Make sure the thread is wound evenly on to the bobbin and that it is not too full of thread. Check also that the bobbin is threaded correctly.

### Loopy stitches

If you are sewing very thick or thin fabric you may need to use a thicker, or thinner, needle and thread. Loopy stitches may also happen if either the top thread, or the bobbin thread is too loose. You can find out on the opposite page how to tighten the threads by changing the tension.

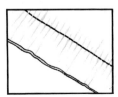

### Puckered fabric

The stitches you are using may be too short, or the tension on the threads may be too tight.

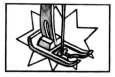

## Machine gets stuck

There may be a bit of thread or fluff caught round the bobbin. Unplug the machine, then check that the bobbin thread is running freely.

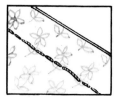

## Missing stitches

This happens when the needle is blunt or not fitted correctly, or if the needle is too thin for the fabric. Check too that the machine is correctly threaded and that the tension on the top thread is not too loose.

## Uneven stitches

This is usually because the tension on the two threads is incorrectly balanced. Alter the tension as described below and keep trying out the stitches on scrap fabric.

## Changing the tension

You can alter the tightness of the top thread and the bobbin thread. It is better though, to alter the tension of only the top thread if possible as it is easier to control.

The tightness of the top thread is controlled by the tension dial.

The tension of the bobbin thread is controlled by a screw.

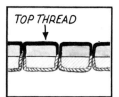

If the tension on both the threads is correct the stitches meet in the fabric.

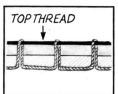

If the top thread lies on top of the fabric, turn tension dial to loosen it.

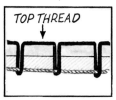

Tighten the tension of the top thread if the bottom thread lies along the fabric.

# Sewing words

**Balance marks**
Dots and triangles on paper patterns which you mark on the fabric to help line up the pieces.

**Basting**
Another name for tacking—long stitches for holding fabric before you sew it properly.

**Bias binding**
Special tape which is cut from fabric at an angle to the straight grain.

**Bodkin**
A thick, blunt needle with a large eye for threading elastic.

**Casing**
The place through which elastic or tape is threaded.

**Easing**
Fitting a larger piece of fabric to a smaller one by gathering it so it is the same size.

**Facing**
A shaped piece of fabric sewn to a neckline or armhole to finish off the raw edge.

**Interfacing**
Stiff material which is put in collars and cuffs, or behind facings to give weight and stiffness.

**Nap**
The pile of fabrics such as velvet, corduroy, velour and fake furs.

**Notches**
Little triangles on dressmaking patterns which you cut round and which help you line up the fabric pieces when you pin them together.

**Notions**
Everything you need, apart from fabric, to make a garment. When you buy a pattern there is a list of notions on the back.

**Petersham**
Stiff tape which can be used for waistbands.

**Pinking shears**
Scissors with special blades for trimming raw edges to stop them fraying.

**Seam allowance**
The distance between the seam line and the edge of the fabric, usually 1.5cm.

**Shirring elastic**
Fine elastic thread for gathering to give elasticity.

**Slip stitches**
Widely spaced hem-stitches.

**Stay-stitching**
Stitching round curved edges of fabric pieces to stop them stretching before they are sewn together.

**Tailor's tacks**
Special stitches to mark information from a paper pattern on to the fabric.

**Template**
Metal, plastic or card shape used as a pattern for cutting lots of pieces the same size, e.g. for patchwork.

**Top stitching**
Stitching on the right side of the fabric for decoration.

# Index